DIRT BIRD

DIRT BIRD

WES STURDEVANT

Dirt Bird
By Wes Sturdevant

Copyright © 2011 by Wes Sturdevant

Title lettering designed by Angela Sturdevant
Cover photography © 2004 by Wes Sturdevant

First Print Edition: August, 2011
First Printing, 2011

Published by:
Story and Media, LLC
5921 Oak Ave
Indianapolis, IN 46219
www.storyandmedia.net

For Angela
the only girl in the world worth stalking

The laughter stopped as soon as Raymond Tate opened the door. The impromptu gathering of his coworkers at the coffee station had evaporated in the time it had taken him to open his office door. He stood there, coffee mug in hand, and watched the doors to four offices down the hall shut behind four anonymous Qual-E-Tech employees. He looked down at his empty mug, then at the empty coffee pot sitting upside down in the drying rack by the sink. Oh well, he hadn't really come out for the coffee.

He closed the door behind him and looked around his cramped office. It was barely big enough to fit his humble little desk and his armless task chair. A fluorescent light hummed and blinked softly above, casting a faintly greenish light on the white cinderblock walls. There was a small square window, but it looked out into the dark scraggly inside of an overgrown juniper bush, and it didn't open.

Raymond set the empty cup on the barren desk, glanced at the manuscript on his screen, and sighed. He couldn't remember the last time he'd talked to anybody at work. It might well have been years. He remembered that there had been an interview, but not much had been said. The HR lady in the shoulder pads had just asked his name, glanced at his résumé, and asked him when he could start. He didn't think she worked there anymore. But then again, if it hadn't been for the paycheck that was automatically deposited into his bank account every two weeks, and the new manuscripts that showed up in his email inbox every few days, he wouldn't even be sure *he* worked there anymore.

Qual-E-Tech made stuff, all sorts of stuff. If it had a cord and you could plug it into a wall and make it do something, like burn toast, or make noise, or flash little colored lights, they probably made some cheap version of it. They didn't develop anything, they just waited for some other company to develop something, then they would buy a few of them at the Circuit City across the street. The team of reverse-engineers, who drove obnoxiously big SUVs, would bring the gadget back, take it apart, and see how it worked. Another team of engineers, who preferred whiny little suped-up sports cars, would then figure out a way to improve the device, like make it burn toast faster, or make louder noises, or flash more little colored lights. They made just enough changes to a device to be able get around any patent issues. The plans would then go to a manufacturing plant in China where Chinese engineers would find a way to make it cheaper by using the worst components they could dig up. The Chinese engineers would then write a manual for the device. They wrote the manuals in simplified Chinese, then had a secretary run it through an online translation service before sending it back. The automated translations were, without exception, completely incomprehensible. Raymond's job was to translate these manuals from pseudo-English into English.

Today his cursor was flashing before a sentence that read: "Do not start the power switch to block the power line until you to enter the wall." This he translated as: "Do not turn the power switch on until you have plugged the power cord into the wall." He had no references to check, no contact with the Chinese engineers or their secretary. He had no background in Chinese or engineering. He did all of his work by intuition, inference, and educated guessing. He had no idea how well he was doing or if his translations were correct. He never got any feedback at all, good or bad. But what difference did it make? For all he knew his laughing coworkers, the ones who never spoke to him, who probably had never even noticed him, were sitting in their own little offices, drinking the last of the coffee, and translating the same exact sentence.

He sighed again and turned his head to stare out the window. The evergreen bush blocked out all sunlight and any view that might lie beyond. He had no idea what was out that window. It had been overtaken by the bush long before he'd started with the company. Two years ago a pair of pigeons had built a nest on the window's ledge, and he had watched for almost two months as they took turns sitting on the small white eggs, and then feeding the hungry hatchlings. He had been amazed at how democratically the work had been split between the hen and the cock. Every day he hurried to work to see how the two little peepers were doing. He watched as they molted from the soft baby down into their beautiful, smooth contour feathers. According to the book he'd bought, they were only a day or two from making their first fledgling flights when he saw the handle of a garden tool poke in through the shelter of the evergreen branches and destroy the nest. He watched in horror as an unseen maintenance man knocked the nest from the ledge. He banged on the window and yelled helplessly as the handle jabbed over and over at the nest, crushing the little peeps. He cried the whole afternoon that day and fell four hours behind on the manual he'd been editing.

Raymond looked at the time flashing in the corner of his computer screen. It was four-thirteen. *Forty-seven minutes 'till quitting time*, he told himself, *forty-seven minutes.*

* * *

Don Peregrine rolled the van slowly down the street. Craning his neck and leaning over the dash, he read the street numbers to himself. *Thirteen-nine, thirteen-eleven, thirteen-fifteen.*

"Goddamn it! Were the hell is thirteen-thirteen?"

He slammed on the brakes and threw the van into reverse. Backing down the narrow one-way street he noticed an alley he had somehow missed. He jammed the van into park, slapped the flasher button, and got out.

The cigar in his mouth had gone cold and sour. He fumbled around in the pockets of his overalls with big dull fingers looking for his Zippo. Finding it in the cargo pocket with the box of Ju-Ju-Bees, he flipped it open and thumbed the steel.

Snick.

Snick.

Snick.

"Come on, you cheap piece of shit."

Snick.

Snick.

Snick, snick, snick, snick!

He threw the lighter through the van's open window. It hit the floor hard, and disappeared amidst a collection of junk food wrappers and plastic vodka flasks. He threw the cigar down and stomped on it. Gritting his teeth, he ground it into the asphalt with his steel-toed boot.

"Fuck! Fuck! Fuck!"

Today wasn't turning out so good. First the shower head had popped off and hit him on the head, and then his wrinkled goat of a wife had burnt the toast. Eighteen years of marriage and the bitch couldn't even get his toast right. He should have shoved the blackened Brillo pads she'd buttered up and tried to serve him down her goddamn—*Breathe*, he told himself, *Breathe!*

He sucked in a big chest full of air, and let his hands hang loose at his sides, just like Dr. Philips had taught him. He closed his eyes and rolled his head around his shoulders, letting the breath out slowly. He counted to ten and thought about his happy place: a blue corduroy Lazy Boy parked under a palm tree on the beach pictured on the air freshener that hung from the van's rearview mirror. He imagined the sound of the waves rolling up on the beach, and the giggles of the bubble-butted brown girls who frolicked topless in the sea foam. The setting sun highlighting their brown curves in orange. He imagined taking a pull from his beer, tasted the lime stuck in the neck of the bottle, and swallowed before opening his eyes to find himself standing in the alley.

A few yards down the alley he saw that there was a second building hiding behind the one that faced the street. It was a crooked little thing with walls that looked too tired to stand up straight. Crumbling mortar bulged out between the pale brown bricks. Greening brass numbers screwed into the peeling doorframe read *1313*.

"Well fuck me sore and kick me out of bed," Don said.

A pretty little thing in a Northwestern sweatshirt opened the door. She used her little pinkie to pull the limp black hair from her face, and squinted up at him like the sunlight hurt her eyes.

"Hello?" she said.

"Ma'am," he said, tipping his baseball cap so she could read the Crosshair Pesticide logo, "Peregrine Pest Control. I got a call for this address."

"Thank god," she said, rolling her eyes in dramatic exacerbation. "Come in."

The apartment was small, dark and cluttered with books and manila folders.

"Excuse the mess," she said, "I'm cramming for the bar exam."

The place was a mess, dirty dishes piled in the sink, cereal boxes sitting open on the counter, a couple of pizza boxes stashed behind the overflowing trash can, but it smelled nice. It smelled sweet and feminine, like powder and lavender.

"I saw it over there," she said, pointing a pink painted fingernail at a spot where the old yellowing linoleum curled up and away from the baseboard of the cabinets.

"Saw what?"

"A big black greasy rat," she said shivering.

It only took a couple of minutes to find the quarter-size hole that had been gnawed into the floorboard inside the cabinet beneath the sink.

"They're coming through there," he said, shining the Mag Light so the girl could see.

"Oh no, he was bigger than that. A lot bigger."

"Rats are pretty flexible, they can squeeze their bodies through any hole they can get their heads through. See the gnaw marks? They're definitely coming through there."

She shivered again, "They?"

"Just like cockroaches, mam. If you see one, there are hundreds you ain't see'n."

"Hundreds?"

"Well, a few dozen at least."

* * *

It wasn't supposed to be this cold in Chicago this time of year, so the people who rushed through the park were clutching the collars of their shirts closed against the chill and stuffing their hands into the pockets of their thin jackets. Raymond was the only one sitting still in the little park with the modest little fountain at its center. No one took any notice of the small man in the grey raincoat who was feeding the meandering collection of pigeons at his feet. Raymond had spent the better part of the hour between five-thirty and six-thirty there everyday for almost two years now—every weekday that is. Saturdays and Sundays he split most of the daylight hours between five or six of the parks on the city's north side, feeding and talking to the vagrant groups of feral pigeons who lived year-round in the Windy City.

After that horrible day, when he'd witnessed the murder of those chicks outside his office window, Raymond had become suddenly aware of the omnipresence of the birds and began to take a special interest in them. He'd checked out a few more books from the library and learned that they were properly of the species commonly known as the Rock Dove, and that they had come to America with the Europeans. Mankind, he'd learned, had shared a symbiotic relationship with the birds for all of recorded history. Not only were the birds good at cleaning up our discarded food, but until quite recently, pigeon eggs were considered an easy source of nourishment.

Raymond flung a handful of the seed he'd brought from home in an arc over the few dozen birds who waddled around his feet, bobbing their heads and cooing.

"So how was your day?" he asked them.

They cooed some more and pecked leisurely at the seed, unaffected by the cold gust whipping through the park that made Raymond's hands feel dry and raw as he reached into the bag for another handful.

"My day?" he sighed softly. "Oh, you all don't want to hear about my day. But thanks for asking."

He sat quietly for a while, listening to the calm purring sounds the birds made, and trying to imagine what they might be talking about. When the bell on the old Greek Orthodox church down the street rang once, marking the half hour, Raymond stood up, and spilled the rest of the seed on the ground, being sure to shake every last one out. He peered into the bag to double-check, folded it up neatly and placed it in his coat pocket, then said, "Well good night all, I've got to go home and spend some quality time with the family. See you tomorrow."

Just over a year ago Raymond had built a small pigeon coop on his roof following some plans he'd found in an old issue of *Competition Birding*, and now had a "family" of his own. The family was made up of fourteen nesting pairs who he visited with and fed every night. He knew them all by sight, but had kept to a strict rule he'd set for himself at the beginning, and had never named any of them. He loved them all, and the time he spent on his roof with them was the happiest, most rewarding part of his day. He was, however, particularly fond of a beautiful caramel-colored hen, who, along with her mate, a dark grey cock who had somehow lost the middle talon on his left foot, had been the first to roost in his coop. He didn't have a name for her, but he thought about her almost as often as he thought about Tia Lynn.

* * *

What people didn't understand about rats was how smart they were. Smart as dogs according to some, and to Don, that made them worthwhile adversaries. Roaches survived by sheer numbers and simple toughness, but they were as dumb as hockey pucks. All you had to do was scatter enough poison and keep your food sealed, and they were licked. Mice were tenacious, but easily trapped, and termites were easy to prevent if you had any common sense at all. Rats, on the other hand, you had to out-think. They were smart enough to recognize and avoid any trap or poison they'd run into before, and could learn from others' mistakes. If they found a dead comrade and could smell a poison on him, they would know to avoid that poison if they ever came across it themselves.

Unlike most of the other nuisance species that people had brought to America—either purposefully or out of careless ignorance—rats were the one widespread pest people had always actively tried to prevent. Extensive measures were taken to ensure that rats, which had been blamed for the Bubonic plague and were known to ruin whole inventories of a ship's stores, could not stowaway on the boats that left European ports. Nonetheless, the rats had found their way onto every continent and island that white man ever set anchor near. The clever little fuckers could even swim, and had been known to climb down anchor chains and paddle with their scaly little tails to new lands of conquest.

The rat problem at 1313 wasn't so bad. Don had seen a lot worse. It looked like they weren't nesting in the building but were making little sorties from another nearby building, or maybe coming up through the storm sewer grate in the middle of the alley. With the landlord's permission and a nice deposit check, he'd be able to seal most of the obvious points of entry and set bait and traps along the walls inside and out. If the girl, and whoever lived upstairs, could keep their places relatively free of exposed food for a while, the critters would get the message and move operations elsewhere.

The best thing about the exterminator business was that if you were any good you could always win the battle, but you would never win the war. No matter how triumphant you had been at one address, your enemy would always rise up down the street where somebody would be more that happy to hire a ronin samurai to fight their battle for them.

Don could imagine this little alley here might provide enough business to pay for that fancy insemination procedure his wife had insisted on. He was heading to the van to get some flyers to stick on neighbors' doors when he saw the three fresh splotches of bird shit on his windshield.

"Pigeons, " he said, looking up and examining the edge of the old building's roof. There was an old iron fire escape that had more than its share of droppings splattered about it. "Fucking dirt birds," Don snarled, gritting his teeth.

* * *

The Western Avenue bus was running late again. When it finally showed up there was a second one tagging along right behind it. Both busses were full, standing-room only. Raymond stood near the door, packed tight between a tall muscular black kid in a pristine white t-shirt that hung to his knees, and a big round Latina who was shaking the handles of a stroller, trying to keep her baby quiet. The black kid in the clown shirt's shoulder kept bumping Raymond in the ear as the bus bounced over the potholes that scarred the pavement. He had on giant headphones that were blaring a pulsing rap song loud enough for everyone on the bus to hear. He had his eyes closed and was nodding his head to the beat as he mumbled the words out loud. For some reason the driver had the heat cranked. The baby in the stroller, who was bundled up tight against the unseasonable weather, was now sweating from the thick human-scented heat of the bus, and was making a slow cranky whining noise that threatened to break into a full-on wail at any moment. Raymond felt very much like he was trapped in an incubator.

He tried to disconnect his thoughts from his discomfort and imagine the cool that was awaiting him on his roof. His family of birds would have returned from their forays in the city and would be waiting for him in the coop. He'd feed them, and talk to them, and check on the status of the eggs in the nests. He was expecting no fewer than twelve godchildren in the next few weeks. He'd spend an hour or so with them, some of that time just sitting on the folding chair he kept up there and watching the birds settle in for the night. At about eight o'clock he'd say good night, and head back down the fire escape ladder to his apartment.

He knew that at eight Tia Lynn, his downstairs neighbor, would call it a day on her studying and start to get ready for work. He would lay in his dry bathtub with his ear to the fiberglass bottom and listen to her shower. She would listen to the radio while she did her long dark hair, blow-drying it briefly, before putting on her make-up. He'd be able to smell the sweet purple smell of her through the funky old building's ventilation. By eight-forty-five she would be bouncing down the steps, and he would watch out his window as she mounted her old *Vespa* scooter, her skirt sliding up above the knees of her strong runner's legs, and her ankles tapering smooth and naked into her pastel pink tennis shoes, before puttering off to the bar. She'd pull a four-hour shift bringing beer and buffalo-wings to college kids and yuppies at a sports bar down in Wrigleyville. He'd wait up for her, sitting in his chair and watching *Star Trek: The Next Generation*, then *Deep Space 9*, then *Voyager*, until just after two AM, when he'd hear the sputter of the *Vespa's* engine. He'd go into the bedroom and lay awake on his futon until he could no longer hear her moving downstairs. Then he'd try to fall asleep without fantasizing about confessing his love to her. Even in his fantasies the absurdity of her loving him was more than he could imagine away, and they always ended with her laughing hysterically at him. No matter how he phrased it or what wild scenario he dreamt up, she always ended up falling down on the floor, clutching her belly, and tearing up, as she shook with laughter. So he'd convinced himself it was better this way, and he spent every night telling himself over and over again that he was content with loving her from afar.

The harsh reality was that they would never be happy together. But that was nothing new for him, he'd never been happy with anybody, and just being near her made him happier than he'd ever been before. He had come to realize that he was to be alone. That was the great challenge of his life. His mother, God rest her soul, had taught him that the Lord gave each and every one of us a unique challenge, but he never gave us one we couldn't handle. Her challenge was living long enough after his father's death to raise Raymond. Raymond's challenge, he knew, was to live a life alone, without meaningful contact with others, but as his mom had said, he was uniquely capable of living the life that was chosen for him. God made each of us to rise above whatever challenge he set in front of us. Raymond was to be alone, but he would make the best of it. He had his pigeons, and he had Tia Lynn. He didn't have her the way most lovers had each other, but if he tried, he would always be able to stay just near enough to her to feel the joy, the warmth, and the light that she emitted. And maybe, one day, he would be able to help her, to protect her from one of the jagged edges of life, to in some way return the love she had unwittingly radiated into him.

* * *

"Fuck me sore," Don said, tipping back his hat and wiping his brow on his sleeve. A biting cold breeze was blowing in out of the west and out toward the lake, but he was a big guy and the climb up the fire escape had been a bitch, so he'd broken out in a sweat.

The coop on the roof was made of rough cut wood and rusting chicken wire that looked like it had been salvaged out of a scrap heap. It wasn't much to look at, but it was chock full of nesting pigeons.

Some people just weren't right in the head. What kind of fucked up did you have to be to not only tolerate the nastiest feathered mistakes God ever made, but build a damn house for them? Like any exterminator or building manager worth their salt, Don hated pigeons. They were the one foe you could *never* beat. Not only would they win the war, but they'd won almost every battle Don had ever faced them in. It wasn't because they were smart, it was because they were damned devil spawn. They were winged demons sent from hell to shit on everything man ever built. They defecated on every one of man's achievements, no matter how sacred, no matter how holy. They infested every nook and cranny of the city, defacing cars and sculptures, monuments and churches, and you couldn't do much about it, they were hard to poison, impossible to scare, they flew, so they were hard to trap, and there were just too damn many of them to shoot. They were vile creatures and they had no place on this earth as far as Don was concerned.

He used the hose he found attached to the spigot by the low brick wall that ran the perimeter of the black-tarred roof and began spraying the roosting pigeons. He pressed his thumb against the hose's nozzle to force the water into a knife-like shot that knocked the birds from their nests, and sent them squawking and flapping madly out of the coop. He had the last of the demon birds out when his cell phone rang.

* * *

The heat, and the smell, and the constant screeching of the sweating baby finally got to Raymond, so he got off the bus two stops early and walked four and a half blocks against a refreshingly crisp breeze.

He turned onto his street, an old brick lane that had somehow escaped being paved over and that most people mistook for an alley, and approached his building from the rear. This was not his normal custom, and he was struck by how small and meek his building seemed from that vantage point. It was a ragged old thing hidden by three apartment buildings that had grown up around it in the past thirty years. These newer buildings, each a tragic design mistake from its respective decade, were at least three stories taller than his and cast shadows on it at all hours of the day, regardless of the season. Initially he'd found it a very sad looking place when he realized he would have to move into the second-story apartment, but the place had grown on him. It felt somehow fitting that he would make his life in the cool and forgotten shadows of the world. Now, as he looked at it, he recognized a strength and a dignity to its weed-like persistence as it refused to wither away in the presence of its domineering peers.

There was a white utility van parked by the building just under the fire escape and Raymond thought that maybe the landlord had finally decided to fix the dryer in the basement. He looked for some markings to confirm his hope, but found nothing except some dents and some blue and red streaks on the side that made it look like it'd been side-swiped by a CTA bus. He was almost around to the front steps when he heard the boat-like grumble-grumble of the blood red Ford Cobra that came rolling on absurdly wide tires over the bricks of the one-way street. Seemingly oblivious to him, the blond guy driving the car pulled up directly between Raymond and the building, almost running over his toes, and forcing him to go around the back of the car to get to the steps.

The guy honked the horn twice, then opened the door and stood by the car, resting his hands on the roof.

"Yo, Tia!" the guy yelled, before noticing Raymond who was slinking up the stairs. He nodded and mumbled a half-hearted, "'sup, man."

Raymond nodded, trying not to make eye contact. The guy was a bit weasely-looking with a sharp nose and long chin, but he was dressed well in a crisp blue shirt and yellow tie, and had golden brown hair that bordered on perfect. Raymond supposed he was what most women would call a "hottie." A *hottie*, that was a silly word. How did words like that catch on, he wondered, as he fished his keys from his pocket.

He'd just slid his key into the lock when the door pulled open and away from him. Tia Lynn stood smiling with perfectly oversized white teeth on the other side, and for an instance his chest felt like it was too tight for his lungs.

"Whoops!" she said, stepping back to let him move past her into the hallway.

He kept his eyes down, muttering, "Sorry," as he squeezed past her, almost shuddering when her hand bumped his side. Looking down he saw that she had her little pink flip-flops on, and that she'd painted her tiny toenails with an iridescent pearly nail polish he'd never seen her wear before. He was reminded of white gumdrops, sparkling with sugar, as she moved out onto the little landing outside the door.

"Hey Kent!" she said waving to the guy with the car. She hopped down one of the steps, then turned suddenly toward Raymond, smiling. "Oh, hey Raymond?"

Time stopped.

The world froze.

Every moving thing locked up like a seized turbine. The world was perfectly still and Raymond was its lord.

She had said his name.

Oh, hey Raymond?—that's what she'd just said, wasn't it? She *did* know his name. She knew it, and she was speaking to him—*Shit, she was speaking to him!*

"Yes?" he blurted, setting the world back into motion.

"Have you seen any rats?" she asked, wrinkling up her perfect pug nose, sticking out her front teeth, and pulling her hands up to her chin, imitating a rodent.

"A rat? No."

"I had one in the apartment," she said, quivering like she'd just swallowed something nasty, "and the exterminator is here." She pointed to the white van. "He asked if anyone else in the building had seen one. I said I didn't know, but you could tell him if you had, okay?" Something about the way her voice went up high at the end made Raymond feel like he was being talked down to, like he was a child or a pet.

"Okay," Raymond said, willing himself to look into her whirlpool blue eyes, eyes that threatened to pull him in and drown him with their beauty.

"Okay, great!" she bubbled, heading down the stairs. "Have fun."

Have fun. Of all the stock parting words in the world those two were the most annoying. *Have fun*. That was something that Raymond was definitely not going to do tonight as he waited up until God knows what time for her to get home. He'd have to know that she was safe, have to know that Kent hadn't done something awful to her, before he'd be able to fall asleep.

Raymond started to lift his hand to wave goodbye, but stopped himself, knowing it would make him look eager and silly. Instead he closed the door, but not all the way. He left it open just a crack and peered out to watch.

Tia Lynn approached the car. Kent moved around to open her door for her. She smiled a bright genuine smile at him that stung Raymond like a slap across the face. Who the hell was this guy, Raymond wondered. He'd never seen him before. She'd never mentioned him to her sister, who she confessed everything to during their almost daily phone conversations.

"So what's the plan?" Kent asked.

"I don't have to be back early," Tia said. "I got someone to cover my shift."

She'd gotten someone to cover her shift? That was something Raymond had never known her to do. One of the things he liked best about her was that, despite her beauty, and despite all of the attention she received from the guys she was always telling her sister about, Tia Lynn never let it get in the way of her studies or work. School always came first, then work, then her workout schedule. She never missed a shift because she couldn't afford to. She worked the late shift at the bar only because the tips were good enough to let her scrape by on just twenty hours a week. She took good care of herself, morning runs around the neighborhood, step aerobics during the winter, and *Tai-Bo* every Tuesday and Thursday at seven-thirty AM. She had no time for boys.

"Fantastic," Kent the hottie said. "So the night is ours."

"All of it," Tia Lynn said as Kent closed the car door.

Raymond squinted through the crack and watched the Cobra growl slowly down the street. He reran the conversation and the situation through his head trying to decipher its meaning until he heard the yelling. It took him a few moments to realize that the yelling was it was coming from the roof.

* * *

Don slapped the cell phone shut.

"Bitch," he said, "Bitch. Bitch. Bitch!" With the last "Bitch" he slammed a claw hammer down on one of the pigeon nests, smashing both of the little white eggs it held. The goo of the eggs dripped in long thick strings from the head of the hammer.

"Bitch!" he said again, closing his eyes and trying desperately to find his happy place. He needed to smell the sea, to taste the Corona and lime, to hear the carefree giggles of his bubble-butted beauties, but he couldn't. They weren't there. The chill spring breeze brought up goose bumps on his bare arms that wouldn't allow the illusion to set in. And that fucking bitch, that cum-sucking whore of a wife, with the nicotine breath he could smell over the damn phone, was blaming him? How the fuck was it his fault she was bleeding? His count was fine. "Low normal," that's what the Doc had said, "low normal." *Fucking normal!*

"Bitch! Bitch! Bitch!" he screamed, bringing his hammer down again and again. He squeezed his eyes against the sting of tears. Goddamn bitch had turned him into a faggoty-assed queer, making him cry like a momma's boy. And all the time screaming, "Bitch! Bitch! Bitch!" and flailing the hammer around the confines of the little pigeon coop, hitting damp particleboard and nest, the spray of water and strings of egg goop flinging about him.

The sound of flapping wings opened his eyes. The goddamn birds were coming back! Still soaked by the dousing he'd given them with the hose, they were no longer afraid of him. Parental instincts he would never feel himself drove them, like soldiers storming a beach, in through the small coop doors.

"Bitch! Bitch! Bitch!" he screamed, swinging the hammer with one hand and grabbing at pigeons with the other.

* * *

Raymond could hear the commotion more clearly as he climbed up the fire escape ladder. Despite his curiosity he climbed carefully as the bucket of feed he was lugging in one hand was heavy.

"Bitch. Bitch. Bitch!" he could hear the man saying. And then there was the banging sound.

Finally reaching the top, he peered over the edge of the roof and saw a big man in overalls and a baseball cap in his pigeon coop. The man's back was to him, and although he couldn't be sure, it looked like he was hammering something. Pigeons were flying about franticly. Raymond was on the roof and walking toward the coop before he realized what the man was swinging his hammer at.

"Stop!" he screamed, rushing forward. "What are you doing?"

The big man swatted at the swarming pigeons as he staggered backwards out of the coop.

"What are you doing?" Raymond cried, seeing the thick mixture of egg and blood drip from the hammer's head. "Stop it!"

The man staggered back a few steps toward Raymond, who screamed when he saw the vicious claw of the hammer catch one of the angry pigeons in the back, and throw it limp and broken to the rooftop.

"Oh God! Stop it!"

Suddenly, as if startled, the man turned and swung the hammer at Raymond, who stepped back out of the way. The man's eyes were red, and wet, and crazy. Desperately, Raymond shoved his hand down into the bucket of feed and flung a handful of the tiny seeds into the man's face.

The man roared in pain, grabbed at his eyes with one hand and, with the other, flung the hammer, which flew through the air and caught Raymond on the forehead just above the eye. Everything flashed bright like flashbulbs as Raymond stumbled backwards. Just before the flashbulbs went dark and the blackness swallowed him up from the inside, he felt himself trip over the low perimeter wall and tumble backwards off of the roof.

* * *

"Fuck me," Don whispered to himself as he peered over the edge of the roof.

The scrawny little guy lying on the fire-escape landing wasn't moving. Half of his face was covered in blood and somebody had dumped a bucket of birdseed on him.

Don himself was covered in blood and the sticky slime of egg. He couldn't exactly say what had happened, he had lost control there for a minute and then found himself curled up on the roof sobbing, the black tar of the roof smelling sweet and radiating the heat of the day's sunshine into his cheek. When he'd sat up he'd found himself splattered with blood and egg, and surrounded by dead and dying pigeons. He hadn't panicked. No, he'd done like Dr. Philips had taught him to. He'd closed his eyes and filled his lungs fully with air. He'd counted to ten, then let it out and found himself sitting in his happy place where he lounged in his recliner and watched the bare-breasted island girls frolic in the waves.

After a few minutes of meditation, he'd stood up, wiping sticky hands on the legs of his overalls, and found that his hammer was missing. Not finding it on the roof, he'd gone to check the fire escape. That was when he saw the scrawny little guy.

"Fuck me," he said again, trying to piece things together in his head.

On the landing Don bent over the guy and reached to touch him, but his hand stopped just short, unwilling to move.

"Hey, buddy," he whispered, "you okay?"

He tried again just a little louder, but wasn't really sure he wanted to know. He pulled his cell phone from the bib pocket of his overalls, and flipped it open, but he couldn't will himself to push the buttons. He looked around and saw how dark it had become. Lights glowed warm and cozy from behind the curtained windows of the apartments next door. His stomach growled, and he longed to be at home, watching TV, and washing down a *Hungry Man* dinner with *Dark Eyes* Vodka. He wanted to be drunk on the couch, flipping through cable channels and listening to his wife snore, so he stood up, took a deep breath, and headed down the fire escape.

* * *

Not long after the exterminator's footsteps had faded away, a caramel-colored hen flapped over the roof's edge and landed gently on Raymond's chest. She cooed softly once, then stood quiet and still for a moment as his chest rose and fell with weak breaths. She stepped forward onto his collarbone and brought her face close to his. She cooed again.

The steady flow of blood from the wound above Raymond's eye was now dripping off the side of his face and onto the grating of the fire escape. The thick red drops hung there like ripening fruit, swelling until they broke free and plummeted, one by one, to the ground below.

The hen spread her wings and flapped them. Her talons tugged at the collar of Raymond's shirt. She flapped and flapped. His head wobbled ever so slightly.

Resting back down on his chest, she cooed loudly three times.

The exterminator's van roared to life somewhere below. Its tires spun, throwing sand and loose gravel as it tore away down the alley.

Presently the hen's mate, the big grey cock with the missing talon, came over the roof and landed next to her. They cooed softly to each other and rubbed necks affectionately, and then he took off and disappeared over the roof's edge. She settled down on Raymond's chest and rode the rise and fall of his breaths.

Her mate was only gone for a few moments. When he returned he was not alone. Half a dozen of their coop mates came fluttering down with him. They landed all around on the fire escape. A few came to rest on Raymond's body. They waddled about, heads jerking, and cooed to each other. They examined his wound with orange-ringed eyes, and one or two of the cocks pecked gently at his hands, hands that had fed them so many times, but now would not move.

More of their coop mates arrived, and with them some of the pigeons who nested nearby.

The caramel hen flapped her wings again and tugged at Raymond's shirt. Her mate and a few others did likewise. The effort was short-lived, but then others took position, gripping his shirtsleeves and pants, and the second effort got his arms and one leg to rise off the landing.

Pigeons began arriving from all directions. Soon there were hundreds of them lining the fire escape, the rooftops, and the power lines, cooing, and flapping, and waddling around. Talons gripped at every square inch of

Raymond's clothes. They gripped his shoelaces, and at his hair, and they strained with the weight of him. Exhausted birds who lost their grip were immediately replaced with others. Flapping, and dragging, and tugging, and pulling in a loosely ordered syncopation, they lifted his limp body just centimeters, but it was enough to move him steadily toward the open window.

It took a spectacular effort to avoid bumping his head as they moved him through the window, but they managed to get him safely on the futon that lay on the floor just inside. Immediately the caramel-colored hen set to work tugging at the bedclothes with her beak. The others followed suit and began arranging the ratty sheets and blankets. Teams of cocks pulled the pillows in close around him as others pulled clothes from an overflowing laundry basket. With care and patience they worked to build the walls of the nest.

Although the night grew cold Raymond was snug beneath the blanket of birds who roosted, with feathers puffed out against the chill, on top of him. In the dark purple hour before sunrise, the songbirds arrived and assembled in the tree by the window to sing a hopeful trilling vigil.

When the sun came up and Raymond still had not stirred, the caramel-colored hen flew out to the landing where she ate some of the spilled seed. After resting again on his chest for a while she crept up to his face and put her beak between his lips. The other birds watched as her stomach spasmed once, and she regurgitated a few ounces of a thin milky substance into his mouth. Reflexes not dependent on consciousness kicked in and Raymond swallowed the nourishing pigeon milk.

* * *

I have ten thousand eyes. Ten thousand points of view search the city for him, looking down every street, waddling around in every dark park, soaring through the canyons of glass and steel and stone. I have eyes perched on cold concrete ledges and on the grotesque stone features of lonely gargoyles. I see thousands of figures walking the streets. I scan thousands of faces. I search and I search—and there he is, walking alone on a deserted sidewalk, holding his stupid hat on and leaning into the wind that's roaring off the lake.

My eyes all shift and begin to converge on him from a thousand different directions. All of my eyes focus on him.

He turns his head and sees me coming for him. His two eyes see the rage in my many eyes, and reflect confusion first, then terror.

He begins to run, his hat flying off and tumbling on the wind down the street. His plastic flask of booze bounces on the concrete as he bolts franticly for cover that does not exist.

I move fast, swooping down on him with hundreds pecking beaks and eight times as many tearing talons. His scream echoes through my many ears before it is lost in the thunder of my wings.

The place stunk of 80-proof piss and industrial disinfectant, the way all subway stations did, but at least it wasn't the body this time. Detective Sean O'Brian had a weak stomach and couldn't really handle the stinkers, so the unused CTA subway platform's odor was rather pleasant considering the alternative.

He wiggled his slippery toes in his damp socks, trying to scratch the itch of the fungus that was eating away at the pale wet flesh between his toes. He'd tried the creams but they just didn't seem to be effective. Wiggling his toes madly, he watched his partner, the legendary Detective Lieutenant James Shank (a.k.a. Slim Jim), a tall, bony man with a waxed handlebar mustache, as he reached into the inside breast pocket of his duster. The long cowboy-style duster with the beef jerky in the pocket was as essential to Slim Jim's image as the big black Stettson he wore on his head. The size thirteen black velcro Reeboks on his feet were the only flaw in his lawman of the West look. There were rumors that he carried a Remington six-shooter revolver, but nobody had ever seen it.

The dead man was face down in a pool of blood on the floor and had an odd hump to his back, like that freaky hunchback in that Disney movie. That movie had made Sean sick, and looking at that hump was making him queasy, so he averted his eyes. Something shiny caught his attention. A quarter glinted up at him from the damp black muck between the two main rails of the train tracks. Sean had often wondered what exactly it would take for him to risk climbing down from the platform. So far he'd decided it would take at least twenty bucks. But seeing as how the trains that normally sped by the retired stop had been rerouted until they could get the body out, he was actually considering going after that quarter.

"Got something there, O'Brian?" Slim Jim asked as he reached into his pocket and pulled out a vacuum-packed stick of hot and spicy beef jerky. He peered over the edge of the studded blue warning strip that people were supposed to stand behind until the train came.

"Ahh, no. Just checking it out." Sean stammered.

Slim Jim pointed at the body with his jerky.

"Stiff's over there, Detective." He used his teeth to rip open the wrapper. "Try to keep up with me boy," he said around the bit of wrapper clenched in his teeth. He tried to spit out the piece of wrapper, but it stuck to his mustache. Keeping up the cool cowboy act, he wiped it away with the back of his hand and adjusted the Stettson in one, almost smooth, move.

They turned their attention to the hunched stiff on the floor. Juan Sanchez, from the Medical Examiner's office, had beaten them to the scene again and was leaning over the body, prodding it with a latex-gloved finger.

"What's the skinny on the stiff, Bobo?" Slim Jim asked.

Sanchez scratched his balding head with that same probing finger and said, "He's dead, Jimmy."

Slim Jim waved the jerky over his shoulder at Sean, "Write that down, detective." Sean knew the man was giving him shit. Not only was Sean the greenest twig in the department, but he was the commissioner's nephew. It was no secret that his test scores hadn't quite merited a spot on the Area Six Violent Crimes squad, and they certainly didn't merit him being assigned as Jim Shank's partner. So what was a guy to do? He pulled out his notebook, touched the tip of his pencil to his tongue, and scribbled, "Deceased found dead."

"Who's the Sarge in charge?" Slim Jim asked.

"Lindsey," Sanchez said, pointing that finger down the platform.

Sergeant Lindsey stepped out of the shadows at the far end of the platform still tugging at his fly. He smoothed the front of his blue polyester trousers and shrugged.

"Detectives," he said, coming forward and extending his hand.

Slim Jim didn't take the hand. He just nodded and said, "Sergeant."

Sean wasn't really in a position to refuse the Sarge's handshake, and had to discreetly wipe his hand on his pants as soon as the men turned their attention back to the body.

"What's the scoop, Sarge?" Slim Jim asked.

"The man's dead."

"Write that down, O'Brian."

Sean bit his lip and ticked off two little ditto marks under the first note.

"Track maintenance guys found him this morning. Thought he was a bum sleeping it off. That was about six. The first officers on scene were pullin' transit duty. They didn't touch nothin'."

Sanchez stood up and snapped a couple of pictures. The flashes made Sean a bit dizzy. Slim Jim chewed on his jerky and asked Sean if he'd gotten all that down. Sean rubbed his eyes and scribbled it down as best he could remember.

"Let's see his face," Slim Jim said to Sanchez, who rolled the body over.

"What the hell?" the Sarge gasped, holding his hand to his face.

"Ouch!" said Slim Jim.

The sight of the man's face, or the mess of red and wet that had been his face, was more than Sean's stomach could handle, and though he tried to hold his mouth shut with his hand, some of the Italian beef he'd eaten for breakfast managed to find a way out through his nose. He stumbled to the edge of the platform, fell to his knees on the painful studs of the warning strip, and spewed the rest of his breakfast onto the tracks. Spicy Gardiniera and bile burned his sinuses, making his eyes water.

"What in Jesus' name is that?" asked Sanchez, crossing himself.

"*That* is disgusting," Slim Jim said, waving his jerky at the man's badly mangled face. "That's what that is."

"Yeah, but what's *that*?" the Sarge asked, pointing at the thing in the man's hands.

Sean wiped his eyes with his sleeve as he walked back to the body. He swallowed hard, tasting the tang of sick in his mouth, and steeled himself for the gore. He wasn't sure if he could stand to see it again, but curiosity was pulling him forward.

"What's he got there, Bobo?" Slim Jim asked.

And now Sean could see what they were talking about. The man, dressed in tattered and bloody overalls, was clutching something in his hands. It was small, soft-looking, and soaked in blood. Sanchez snapped a photo and leaned over to inspect the thing. With that gloved finger he touched it, causing the thing's head to role over. It stared up at them with tiny orange-ringed eyes.

"I think," Sanchez said, "I think it's a pigeon."

* * *

For nearly a week none of the pigeons returned to their coop to sit on their ruined nests. They did not go sit atop the rotting remains of their eggs. They had a new home now, a new nest to sit on and a new mouth to feed. Day and night they took turns nursing Raymond back to health, splitting the work evenly between the hens and the cocks. Slowly the milk they pushed between his lips thickened, the seeds became less and less pre-digested, until it was a thin gruel of barely softened seeds.

Then one day, quite without warning, Raymond's eyes popped open. He sat up in his nest, causing the startled birds to flap about a bit, stretched his arms, and yawned. He threw his legs over the wall of his nest and put his feet to the floor, which was very cold. Casually, but gently, he pushed pigeons out of the way until he found his slippers, then he padded out of the bedroom and into the bathroom to brush the foul taste out of his mouth.

Looking in the mirror, he was as surprised to find the healing gash above his eye, as he was to find that he had grown a beard. He did not look at his watch, or glance at the clock while he dressed. He did not question why the milk he poured over his *Grape-Nuts* had gone bad, nor why he actually didn't mind eating two bowls of the cereal dry.

* * *

An unfriendly and homely looking young lady led Slim Jim and Sean down the narrow halls of the Field Museum's exhaustive fauna collection. Strange creatures, each forever frozen in some iconic pose, lined the long shelves at either side. As their guide through the labyrinth of halls and chambers that ran, endlessly it seemed, beneath the museum made no attempt at identifying any of the glassy eyed creatures that stared down on them, Slim Jim took it upon himself to supply his own wild conjectures.

"I'll reckon," he said, yanking the jerky he was gnawing on from his mouth and wiggling it at a stuffed bird that had long straw-like legs and a sharp bill, "that critter there is one of 'em Long-Billed Ding-Dongs." The girl was not amused and simply picked up her pace.

"They're creeping me out," Sean said, adjusting his grip on the small blue Igloo cooler. It was emblazoned with a day-glow orange sticker that warned that the contents of the cooler were "EVIDENCE: To be handled by authorized persons only!"

Their guide stopped abruptly and rapped with two big knuckled fingers on a windowless door.

"Yes?" inquired a man's voice from the other side of the door.

"They're here, Doctor Prattle," their guide said, continuing briskly down the hall without so much as a word to the detectives.

"Ornery pole cat," Slim Jim commented under his jerky seasoned breath.

The door swung inward to reveal Dr. Joseph Wilson Prattle, a very hairy man in a worn and stained brown sweater vest and yellowed t-shirt. Giant blue eyes bulged out at the detectives through round spectacle lenses nearly as thick as they were round. He flashed a crooked toothed grin through a wild tangle of red beard whiskers. At first Sean assumed that the man was very short, but soon realized that he had not bothered to stand up to open the door but had just rolled over in his old green desk chair.

"Yes, yes, please come in," the Doctor insisted, pushing off the doorframe with his feet and rolling back to his cluttered desk.

Sean already didn't like the guy. He had on those all-terrain sports sandals and the nubbly white toes with the tuffs of wiry red hairs were enough to give Sean the willies. As far as he was concerned, toes were not for public viewing.

"Thank you kindly," Slim Jim said, taking off his tall cowboy hat and ducking slightly to pass through the low doorframe.

"Have a seat," the man said, waving at a threadbare couch. "How can I help you?"

"Well, Doc," Slim Jim said, pulling the *Zip-Lock* freezer bag from the cooler Sean had set between them. Inside the bag was the slowly thawing, but still stiff body of the bloody bird they'd found clutched in the dead hands of Don Peregrine. "What can you tell us about this poor guy?"

The doctor took the bird and without breaking the bag's seal said, "Well, I can tell you he's dead."

"Write that down O'Brian."

Sean bit his lip in frustration as he pulled the notebook from his pocket.

"He's got a broken neck," the doctor continued, turning the bird upside down and squinting at it, "and he's not a he, he's a hen."

"What manner of foul is she, Doc?

"Common feral Rock Dove."

"We figured it for a pigeon."

"One and the same, Detective, one and the same," the man said, holding the bag up to the light and squinting through his glasses at the bird. "Is all this blood hers?"

"It's mostly the victim's blood."

"The victim?"

"The bird was found in the hands of a dead man —an exterminator, fittingly enough. Found him face down in a pool of his own juices. Best as we can tell he was attacked by a pack of pigeons."

"That's highly unlikely. Pigeons are not aggressive animals."

"We figured, him being an exterminator and all, maybe he got 'em all riled up, and they kind of just went crazy on him."

"I don't think you could get them that excited."

"Have you ever heard of any attacks?"

"Not on an adult, and nothing more than a startled bird scratching a child while trying to fly away. Where were the bird and the deceased found?"

"On the platform of an unused subway station."

"Underground?" the doctor asked in disbelief.

"Yup, the Taylor stop," Slim Jim said shrugging.

The doctor's buggy blue eyes looked to Sean as if to confirm what he'd heard. Sean just nodded and looked back at his notes.

"Well," said the doctor, "that is highly unusual. Do you think maybe the body was moved?"

"It don't seem likely. There were some blood smears on the walls leading down to the platform, but there was also a lot of feathers on the platform, and some droppings too. Seemed like there might have been quite a pack of birds in that place."

"What about after he was dead?" Sean blurted, suddenly struck with a horrifying vision of frenzied pigeons feeding on the face of the dead man. "I mean if the pigeons found the guy already dead, maybe bleeding from the face, might they have started feeding on him?"

"Certainly not," the doctor said, waving away the possibility with both hands. "They're not scavengers, they're foragers."

"Could they be trained?" Slim Jim wanted to know.

"To attack? They're very smart birds, but you'd have to train them against their instinct. They haven't survived this long by being confrontational. Like most birds they tend to just fly away from dangerous situations. I don't think you'd be able to turn them into killers."

"You got any ideas about how our guy might have ended up all tore up by pigeon claws, beaks, or whatever, Doc?"

"Well, I'd be happy to do some looking around, call some colleagues, but I've got to tell you, Detectives," the doctor said, stroking his wild red whiskers. "I just can't make any sense of it."

"Neither can we, Doc," Slim Jim said, getting up and carefully positioning the Stetson on his head. "Neither can we."

* * *

Raymond knew that the Cobra was coming before he could hear it. He didn't have to get out of his nest to know that Tia Lynn was in the passenger seat. He knew that she'd gotten in the car with Kent after the bar review lecture downtown in the west Loop, and that they had stopped at a Greek joint for lunch. He'd seen her from above and below as she came giggling and a little bit tipsy out of the restaurant. And watched her long dark hair play in the wind as they drove up Western with the top down, reveling in the beauty and warmth of the day.

Now he was rolled up in a tight little ball, hugging his knees, as he listened to the sounds of them fucking below him. And though he had his eyes closed tight against the stinging tears he could see her through the billowing sheers of her bedroom window, arching her back and pushing her perfect breasts forward for Kent to kiss. It was the look of genuine love-fueled bliss on her face, the wide open mouth, closed eyed smile, seen from a dozen slightly different angles, that cut him like a box knife drawn slowly and repeatedly across his heart.

* * *

I didn't have to spread our wings to follow him. From eyes perched above every street, I could track every move he and his loud, compensating-for-something, car made. I watched as he rolled from Tia Lynn's bed, out to the car, and then directly to the townhouse in Lincoln Park. My many ears heard him honk that horn of his and call out for her. I watched another girl, with her blond curls and high-heeled sandals, come precariously down the stairs. At the restaurant they sat outside enjoying the warm evening. I bobbed my heads and pecked at the crumbs of tortilla chips he threw to me from his plate, and watched his hand go up her skirt and stay there while the embarrassed waitress brought them a third round of margaritas. All the while my other eyes watched Tia Lynn sleep in the bedroom below me, dreaming post-coital dreams of happily ever after.

I was waiting for Kent and the other girl when they arrived back at her place, and watched as he slapped her ass and called her a lush while she tried drunkenly to find her keys in her tiny purse. And as he pushed her, cackling at the top of her lungs, through the door I realized that I would have to wait there, all night maybe, for him to come out. But that was okay, it would be worth it to see the look on his face, and to hear him scream.

* * *

Kent bounded down the front stairs of the three-story Lincoln Park townhouse. It was a gorgeous day. Fresh blue sky peeked down on him through the green leaves of the old trees whose thick knobby arms arched over the narrow street, casting diffuse shadows on the pavement. This was the kind of morning that made Kent want to whistle. He was a bar and a half into *Bad to the Bone* when he became conscious of his morning breath and popped a piece of *Trident White* into his mouth.

He checked his watch. He didn't have time to go home. He looked down, touching his chin to his chest, and examined his clothes. The starch in his shirt had given out, but the suit looked good enough for work. His deodorant might give out toward the end of the day, but he had some cologne in the Cobra's glove box.

He pulled two pairs of balled-up panties, one from either pocket, and held them up to his tie. The candied pink of Tia Lynn's high-legged briefs matched the accent stripes in his spring green tie better than the red satin thong of the girl whose apartment he'd woken up in did. *What was her name again?* He sniffed the thong. It smelled like ass. He stuffed it back in his pocket. Then he sniffed the pink ones, they smelled like lavender. *Nice,* he thought, carefully tucking the panties into his jacket pocket so that they looked like a handkerchief, *I might just have to see that girl again.*

It was too bad in some ways that he didn't have time to stop by the condo. It would have been fun to come in the back door where his brother and their roommate would be eating *Pop-Tarts* and drinking *Red Bull.* If he knew them, it would be about eight seconds before they spotted the panties in his pocket and held up their hands for the high-fives. But he'd leave them hanging just long enough to pull the thong out of his pocket and swing it around like a pistol on his finger. Then his little bro would pull one of the chairs out into the middle of the room and make him sit so they could start grilling him for the details. He'd play innocent: "I swear they were planted on me." But they were lawyers too, and they actually practiced in court—unlike him who had used his degree to get a cushy job scoping law students as site manager for a bar review company—so they would start in with the questions. He would play along, giving half-truths and evasive answers, until he had them foaming at the mouth. But all that could wait until tonight. Besides, by then he'd have the "True-Playa" badge of honor of spending the day soaking in the juices of two students while flirting with half a dozen others he'd been working on. Hell, the day was young; maybe he'd make it three—

His blood ran cold like Freon.

The Cobra was where he'd left it, but it was not *how* he'd left it. His fire-engine red chick magnet was the color of moldy oatmeal. It was covered—headlights to custom-tuned, split-exhaust, chrome tailpipes—with a glistening layer of fresh bird shit so thick and even that a passerby would never have been able to guess the color of the paint job that was being permanently ruined beneath it.

With the disbelief of a child seeing his dad dressed up like Santa Clause, Kent looked up and down the row of cars that were parked bumper-to-bumper on either side of the street. Each and every one of them was completely and utterly free of droppings of any size or sort.

Burning rage engulfed him like it had been spit from a flamethrower. He clenched his fists tight, threw back his head, and screamed until his throat was raw.

He never noticed the big grey cock on the low garden wall across the street. The bird watched him with orange-ringed eyes and tiny ears that were seeing and hearing for his many accomplices who were now out of range of the man's hoarse cry.

* * *

The men's room at the Area 6 police station always smelled of stale cigarette smoke and dull old farts. Sean had waited at his desk until he was reasonably sure there was nobody in the restroom before going in to relieve himself. Before entering he'd had to go so bad that he was wiggling in his chair. Now that he was in front of the urinal he couldn't go to save his life. It didn't help that he wasn't alone. The door to the only working stall was closed and he could hear the rustling of a newspaper coming from the other side. With the stall taken he'd had to settle for the third urinal, the one farthest from the door and right up against the wall.

He hadn't always had a shy bladder, but once at a White Sox game he'd stepped up to the urinal in a crowded seventh-inning-stretch men's room and, for some reason, could not do it—not with all of those guys standing behind him waiting their turn. After that shake of confidence he'd developed a bit of a complex.

Today things weren't so dark, he didn't have the place to himself, but at least nobody was watching him, and if he hurried he could get it over with before anyone else came in. He had a trick, a ritual to coax things along. He had to relax and put his mind on something else, so whenever he found himself struggling in some nasty restroom he'd focus on planning how exactly he was going to escape the room without touching anything but himself. The station's restroom was easy, he'd done it a thousand times. All he had to do was get a paper towel before washing his hands, use the towel to turn the water on and off, then use it again to work the lever on the dispenser and get another towel to dry his hands. He'd use that same towel to push open the bathroom door, which was double-hinged and swung both ways like a kitchen door at a restaurant, and either make a bank-shot off the wall and into the trash can or just throw the towel in the wastebasket at his desk.

Things were moving down there, and he was relieved to feel the first sting of success when the double-hinged door squeaked slowly open. *Aw, hell,* Sean thought, turning his head to see Slim Jim saunter into the room using one hand to push open the door. His eyes took in his surroundings like a marshal stepping into a saloon.

"Howdy pardner," he said. "I reckon I've swaller'd enough joe to drown a buffalo."

The guy in the stall let out a little toot and the cowboy replied, "Afternoon, Jones."

"How's it going, Shank?" a gruff voice rumbled from behind the stainless steel stall door.

Great, Sean thought as Slim Jim stepped up to the urinal closest to the door. Now he was either going to have to stand there until his partner left, or zip up and pretend he was done. Unsure, he hesitated so long that he realized he'd missed his window of opportunity. It would look weird if he left now, he'd have to stand there.

The tall man put one hand on the wall above the urinal and leaned into it. Sean kept his eyes straight ahead and tried to bore a hole into the gray tiles on the wall while he listened to the sound of the man opening his big silver belt buckle and pulling down his zipper with his free hand. Immediately there was the whisper of streaming water.

"Ahh," Slim Jim sighed.

Sean closed his eyes to see the silhouetted image of a well-endowed buffalo, back lit by the glowing rays of a brilliant sunset, relieving himself with a thick gushing golden stream on the top of a grassy hill.

Just then the door squeaked open again. Sean kept his eyes shut and silently cursed his luck.

"Detectives," a familiar voice greeted them. Sean opened his eyes to see Chief Sato step up to the open urinal between them. "How's the Peregrine case going?" Sean thought the man looked like a happy Buddha statue with a comb-over.

"Well, to be honest sir," Slim Jim admitted, "it's a real stubborn bitch."

"Catch me up. What do we know?" A second stream started to tinkle, while the first kept gushing.

"We're thinking maybe it wasn't the birds. Maybe someone just kilt him, then disfigured the body."

"With a pigeon?"

"With a beak and some claws. Maybe the perp made some sort of tools with 'em?"

"Anybody hate this guy?" said the Chief, zipping up his fly and stepping back from the urinal.

"He wasn't popular. Had anger management issues according to his wife."

"But, you don't like her for it?" the Chief asked, going to the sink and leaning back against it without flushing or washing his hands.

"Naw, they had a fight that night about some medical stuff, he stormed out to get a drink, and she spent the night bitching on the phone to her mother." Finally he stood up straight, shook himself, and zipped up. "Phone records check out." He did up his big round buckle, stepped back, and high kicked the flush handle.

"So what's next?" the Chief wanted to know.

Slim Jim went to wash his hands and shrugged, "We're up a dry creek with a paddle and a speedboat, but no pot to piss in."

The complete and utter nonsense of Slim Jim's analogy didn't seem to phase the Chief, who turned to Sean and asked, "You got any ideas, detective O'Brian? Or should we just file this one under X?"

This must have been the definition of "being on the spot." Maybe they were just razzing him. Maybe it was some sort of a test. "Umm..." his mind raced, "We could start re-interviewing people. Start with the people who saw him on that day. Retrace his steps. Maybe we missed something." It was lame, but it was all he had.

"You think you missed something Jim?"

"There's a first time for everything, I reckon."

"Well get to it then, ladies," the Chief said, walking out of the room.

Slim Jim dried his hands on the thighs of his jeans. "I say we skip the wife, we already tapped that tree. Let's start at the liquor store, and then call on the pretty little thing with the rat problem."

Sean nodded in agreement, praying that the guy would just get the hell out. But he went back to the mirror and examined his mustache. Using two fingers he twisted one of the waxed handlebars into shape, and then tightened his bolo tie.

"Take your time there, boy," he said, finally sauntering through the door. "It's only a murder case."

The blessed sting returned before the door had stopped swinging back and forth on its loud hinges. Sean sighed gratefully, but a sudden reverberating fart from behind the stall door chased his timid relief back up its tunnel.

* * *

The folding chair was cold against Tia Lynn's legs. The nylon running shorts and long-sleeved t-shirt she'd been wearing while studying weren't warm enough for the pre-storm chill that blew over the rooftop. One of the chair legs was shorter than the others, or maybe the roof was just uneven, because the chair kept rocking every time she shifted her weight. She tried to stay very still. She didn't want to make Raymond any angrier.

"Sit," is what he had said, "I have something to tell you."

He looked crazy with his hair all shaved off and that nasty wound above his eye. She'd never seen him like this. He was all dressed up in a crisp white dress shirt that was buttoned up tight around his neck and tucked into new-looking black fatigues. The baggy pants billowed out just below the knees where they were tucked into high-laced maroon colored combat boots. He wore a long, dark grey raincoat with two wide black stripes painted on either side that started in the front near the waist and ran down and back, all the way to the tips of the split tails. The coat was closed around his chest, but open from his waist down, and the tails flapped around behind him like wings. Around his torso, outside the coat, he had this mole grey harness thing that looked like it might have come from an army surplus store. The costume would have been funny if he hadn't been holding that hammer.

So she would sit there, and she would listen if that was what he wanted. That's all she could do, right? She couldn't scream, he'd be able to use the hammer before anyone could get there. He didn't seem to be afraid of being seen, he'd taken her to the roof where anybody in the apartment building across the street could see them. Surely somebody would see them—a man dressed like a pigeon with a hammer, and a woman tied to a chair? Surely somebody would see and get help, and maybe she'd be ok if she could just keep him from getting too mad.

"But first," he was still talking, "I want to show you something."

He wanted to show her something. That's what he'd said when he'd come knocking on her door. He had something on the roof he wanted to show her. He'd been as meek and quiet as he always was when they met in the hall, or in the laundry room, him always fidgeting, averting his eyes and talking into the floor. She usually felt sorry for the poor guy, and would have humored him today when he surprised her by coming to the door, but she'd had so much studying to do that she'd said, "Sorry, some other time maybe."

That's when everything changed. There was an orange flash around the pupils of his eyes that, for the first time ever, were staring directly into hers. She noticed the freshly shaved head and the brown-crusted wound above his eye, and knew that something was off.

"Some other time," she said again, smiling and trying to look friendly while closing the door in the guy's face, but he stomped his foot in the doorway so she couldn't get it shut. That's when she caught a glimpse of the hammer behind his back.

"I'm sorry," he said, stepping into the apartment, "but this is important—very important—and I don't have much time."

He'd tied her hands in front of her with a long red bootlace and used it like a leash to lead her to the roof. She was scared and obedient, but not in a panic. The guy was outright puny. She was almost a foot taller that he was and probably outweighed him by 20 pounds. With three years of Tai-Bo under her belt she thought she could probably take the guy if it came to that.

She'd never been on the roof, so she glanced around. The sun was going down and some of the windows of the three taller apartment buildings that surrounded their little old building glowed with the warmth of incandescent lights and the flicker of televisions. The roof's uneven surface was covered with peeling tar sealant speckled with white bird droppings and some scattered birdseed. She'd known about his pigeons, but had never seen the coop. It was in the corner of the roof and was bigger than she had imagined, large enough to stand in. It looked like it had been built out of salvaged wood with rusting chicken wire and a roof of corrugated metal. To her surprise it was empty. Maybe that was what he'd wanted to show her.

So she was sitting, as she'd been told, and he was kneeling down by the chair. He was about to tie the bootlace to the leg of the chair when he paused and looked up at her. "Sorry, but I ah..." At a loss for words, he shook his head and loosely wrapped the lace around the leg a few times, then let it hang loose. "Is that okay?" It was like he was asking for her permission or something.

She didn't answer. She just stared down at him, anger setting into her face, pulling at her brows, and diluting the fear.

He stood up suddenly, like he'd heard something and closed his eyes. He was still for a moment as if listening to a far away sound she couldn't hear.

'They're close," he said, opening his eyes finally. "We don't have much time."

He moved a few steps in front of her, flipped the tails of his coat out behind him and held up his hands, gripping the hammer by the head, as if he were not going to hit her with it. It looked like a pose he'd practiced in the mirror. He took a deep breath and was still, like he was preparing to do some sort of stupid human trick. He dropped his head and shook it slowly like a man defeated.

"I should have written this down," he said. He closed his eyes and was still for a moment then said, "Okay, okay yeah." He opened his eyes and looked at her. "Tell me what you think about pigeons."

"What I think? I—I don't really."

"Exactly. Nobody does. Umm... Okay. Now, what about me?"

"What?"

"What do you think about me?"

She looked at the hammer, and didn't answer. He followed her gaze and looked a little surprised to find the hammer in his hand.

"Okay, right, right." He put the hammer behind his back, holding it in both hands, and began pacing in front of her. "So how long have we been neighbors?"

"You moved in like a week or two after I did. Like two years,maybe?"

"Right, and before that?"

"What?"

"Before that."

"Before?"

"See, you didn't even notice."

"I lived in Evanston, on Rid—"

"Ridge," he finished her sentence, "819. Apartment B2."

"Oh, my god," she said, not meaning to say it out loud.

"I was B3. Three years living next to you, and you never even noticed me."

"I...I..." she stammered.

"No. No. That's not what this is about," he said. "We're not here to talk about you and me. I just wanted to talk about the things people don't notice—the things around us. We just go about our business and never look around to see. It's like the pigeons, I mean we see them, everybody sees them, they're everywhere, all around us. But people don't see them the right way. They see them like bugs, like pests. Rats of the sky, right? But that's not fair to the rats or the pigeons." The guy was pacing again, trying to find the words.

"Do you know why people hate rats?"

She didn't want to risk an answer. He looked at her with those eyes, and she was scared that she'd have to see that crazy orange flash again so she quickly looked away. Her eyes fell to her feet and she noticed that her toes were curled up tight, pressing hard against the thin soles of her pink flip-flops.

"Well, do you?" he demanded.

She shrugged.

"It didn't always used to be that way. It was the plague. It used to be, before people started dying, that people liked rats. They liked rats, and thought cats were pests. I saw a wood carving in a book once of a giant rat holding up two dead cats by the tails. See, rats were a good omen. If you went into a town and saw rats running around, it was a good sign. If they had rats that meant they had food, they weren't starving."

Tia Lynn grimaced at the thought. Raymond shook his head like she was stupid or something.

"They weren't eating the rats. If they had rats it meant they had enough food stored up for the rats to survive. If there was no food stored, there were no rats. But people are lazy and as towns got bigger, denser, they threw their trash in the streets. The rats had a heyday until there were too many of them. Then came the plague, but it wasn't the rats. It was the fleas, the fleas that lived on the rats. It wasn't the rats' fault they were immune. People didn't know it was the fleas, they thought it was the rats, so they vilified them."

This was crazy talk, this guy really was nuts. She'd made a terrible mistake thinking that she could handle him. Three years of Tai-Bo was no match for a psychopathic whack-job with a hammer.

The sound of a car with a big engine approaching the front of the building rumbled up from below. Raymond went to peer over the edge.

"They're here," he said. "Too soon, too soon."

She heard the sound of two car doors opening, then slamming shut. There were voices mumbling, and she wanted to scream, to call out for help. She opened her mouth, but she had no air—somewhere along the line she must have forgotten to breath. She willed her lungs to suck in air, but her muscles froze as soon as he turned to stare at her. He pointed the hammer at her and held one finger to his mouth. She closed hers.

"I guess now's the time, huh?" he whispered, stepping closer and hiding the hammer behind his back. "I have something to show you." He smiled like a syringe wielding doctor trying to calm an anxious child. "Don't be scared."

He stepped back, striking the same pose he had at the beginning of his rant, and closed his eyes. He held his hands in the air, and was very still. A gentle wind blew over the roof and played lightly, like cold creepy fingers, on the back of her neck.

A caramel-colored pigeon fluttered down from out of the grey sky to land in front of him. Then a second bird, a fat grey one, fluttered down and began hopping around on a gimpy red foot that was missing a toe. A few more birds landed near her chair. Within moments pigeons began arriving from all directions. They flapped and swooped in from behind her, they came in from either side, and dropped down from the grey sky that churned with unnatural energy. Hundreds came to rest on the rooftop; they began lining the windowsills and ledges of the surrounding buildings. The roof was completely covered with meandering pigeons. They waddled around, shoulder to shoulder. Tia Lynn pulled her knees up and her feet off the ground as the birds closed in on her. Overtaken with fear, her rational mind surrendered control of her body and she screamed!

Raymond's eyes popped open. "No!" he cried. "No. It's okay. We won't hurt you."

* * *

The scream sounded like it was coming from the other side of the door. Slim Jim used one of the long black Reeboks to kick it in. He hit it squarely next to the knob. He was tall and skinny, but he was not weak, and he'd misjudged the strength of the doorframe, which splintered like balsa wood. The door flew open, banged up against the wall inside the apartment, bounced back, and slammed shut again.

"Whoa Nelly!" Slim Jim said, looking over his shoulder at Sean. "Reckon I don't know my own strength."

With the toe of his shoe he gently nudged the door back open and slid his hand under his duster. Sean heard the snap of a holster and thought he might just get a glimpse of Slim Jim's fabled revolver, but the man's hand came back from under the coat empty. Sean reached for his own piece. The strap gave him some trouble and by the time he'd wriggled the gun out of the holster, Slim Jim had already stepped into the apartment. They had come up to the second floor apartment after finding the door to the girl's apartment standing wide open and her not around.

"Freaky," Slim Jim said.

Sean took a deep breath and stepped forward. Gun in hand, he peered around the busted doorframe.

"Ain't this some crazy ass shit?" Slim Jim asked, turning around slowly to take in the sight.

The tiny apartment was a disaster. It looked like it had been abandoned and that a whole friggin' flock of pigeons had taken up residence, thrown one hell of a party, then abandoned it. Feathers and a yellow crust of shit covered every surface. It dripped like dried wax from the tops of the cupboards that hung on the wall in the tiny corner kitchenette. It coated the counters and the sad little three-legged table up against the wall. The floor was thick with it. A worn orange armchair by the window was only protected by a plastic cover that reminded Sean of his mother-in-law's living room, and the old TV that sat across from it looked like some sculpture in a park, all streaked with droppings. The shelves on the little bookshelf by the bathroom door looked like they had been nested in by a half dozen birds, with bits of twig and twisted shreds of plastic bags molded into loose, uneven rings.

Other than the feathers, and the shit, and ruined furniture, the room was empty. Sean sucked in a deep breath of relief. A thick moist stench like ammonia and salt made the bile rise up in Sean's throat. "God, I'm going to be sick," he said and slapped his hand over his mouth.

"What, again?" Slim Jim asked, throwing back his head in disgust, "Damn boy, but if you ain't got the stomach of a girl."

Sean made it to the toilet in time, but opted to vomit in the sink because the mess of feathers and muck in the toilet was too gross even to puke on. He was careful not to touch his lips to the crusted-over faucet as he rinsed his mouth out. After spitting in the sink and wiping his mouth on his sleeve, he called out, "Hey, check this out. I think they were using the commode as a birdbath."

"No, son," he heard Slim Jim say in a quiet tone that made his stomach seize up again with dread, "I think you'd best come and check *this* out."

He found his partner in the cramped bedroom standing over a frameless futon that took up most of the floor space. The thin, ratty mattress was covered with a layer of soft downy feathers and the pillows and sheets had been pushed up on the sides with piles of crumpled clothes to form thick nest-like walls.

"Who lives like this?" Slim Jim wanted to know. "Big Bird?"

"Is that blood?" Sean asked, pointing to a dark brownish stain on the futon.

But before Slim Jim could answer, they heard the girl shriek again! Their eyes darted to the open window at the head of the bed and Slim Jim snapped into action. Tromping over the nest thing's walls with his big black sneakers he stuck his head out the window.

"There's more blood here on the ledge, and some on the fire escape. Come on boy, let's get hustlin'!"

And with that, the long slinky detective slid out the window like a snake in a raincoat. Sean was still trying to get his feet to move when he heard Slim Jim start up the ladder.

* * *

Tia Lynn was still crying. Raymond wanted to tell her, they weren't going to hurt her. She had nothing to be sacred of. The hammer was just for show, just so she would come, just so she would listen.

"Tell me, Tia Lynn. What do you know about pigeons?" Raymond asked. He could tell the poor girl was having trouble breathing, let alone talking, but this was important and they didn't have much time, so Raymond stepped closer, holding the hammer by the handle. "Tell me one thing."

Nearly frantic she blurted out, "They live in the park."

"No, they go there to eat." He held up a scolding finger. "They go because *we* go to the park to feed them.

Just like the rats, they wouldn't be here if it wasn't for us. We brought them here. Did you know that?"

She didn't answer. She wasn't focusing. He knew that it must have been hard on her, it was a lot to take in, but he had to get her attention so he yelled, "DID YOU?"

She shook her head, beginning to sob softly again.

"They have always been with us. They followed us from Africa as we conquered the globe. They were with us before the dog, and they will always be with us. Do you know why?"

She shook her head again—good, she was listening. He could soften his tone.

"Because they love us," he said softly. He wanted to tell her that they loved her, that *he* loved her, but he wasn't going to be himself for very long, the change was just moments away, and there was so much she would have to understand.

"Did you know that, after the flood, the dove that went out and brought the olive branch back to Noah was a pigeon? The white dove of peace, the bird of love, is just a white pigeon. They are messengers from God, Tia—our guardian angels. They are full of love for us and they want to show us the way to God, but we won't listen. We're too busy being alone. The problem is we only think individually—no matter how many friends we have, how close we are to our lovers, we're still alone in our heads. Every fucking one of us is an island. Did you ever stop to think that maybe they know more about us than we do of them? We put a monkey in a cage and test it. We drop a rat into a maze and time it. But we never learn anything. We never consider that maybe they think in the same way they survive, as a community—as a whole. One rat may not be so smart, or one monkey, or one bird, but what about all of them? They are always watching us—watching from everywhere—when we are convinced we are alone. And they are thinking—thinking together. Call it instinct. Call it the hive mind. That's how they survive, and how they're gonna survive longer than us."

Raymond stopped to take a breath. He'd been talking too fast to breath. The caramel-colored hen cooed softly, encouraging him to continue.

"But we have it too," he said, "We're not so different, except we keep fighting our instincts. We keep trying to be the individual, the top of the class, the one mommy loves best, and it's what causes all of the problems, all of the hate, all of the pain. Don't you see that's what this is all about?"

Tia Lynn was listening, but he could tell that she didn't understand. She kept looking at him like he was going to attack her, like he was crazy. They would have to show her something, something that would make her understand.

The caramel hen fluttered up and landed on her shoulder. Tia Lynn freaked out and shrieked again. The hen tried to rub necks, but Tia just broke into quivering tears so Raymond reached out his hand and the hen flapped over to him, landing in the palm of his hand.

"No. Don't cry. Please don't." The hen walked up his outstretched arm and they rubbed necks. "See? It's okay. She just wanted to let you know that we aren't going to hurt you. We just want you to understand. I need you to know so you can tell people and make them understand. I wish you could come with us, but you see, I'm the one. I'm the one they need. I'm the one that can make it happen. They've been waiting so long, but now *I'm the one*, and it's going to happen soon. And it will change everything!"

* * *

Sean wiggled himself out of the window and stood on the fire escape landing. Slim Jim was already flying up the ladder, his sneakers squeaking on metal rungs that had been worn smooth with use. Sean was not one for heights, but the rushing adrenaline kept a fresh wave of queasiness in check—that and the fact that he'd just puked his guts out three minutes ago.

He was already starting up the ladder when he felt the dizziness set in. He tried to focus on the bony ass of his partner above him and told himself not to look down, but at the edge of his peripheral vision the rooftops of the surrounding buildings seemed to be moving. He dared not chance a sideways glance to confirm the illusion until he reached the top of the ladder, where he paused, hands gripping the railing that curved over the roof's edge, and looked around.

It had been no illusion. The rooftops *were* moving, alive with uncountable numbers of pigeons. The things were everywhere, lining the roofs, and windowsills, and rear porches. They perched in bobbing lines on the telephone poles and on the power lines that ran down the alley. Above him huge flocks of the birds spun, swirled, and flapped against the low dark clouds. The grey clouds, under lit by orange street light, were moving in fast off of Lake Michigan and, like the birds, they swirled and twisted about angrily. The layers of chaotic motion above brought on the dizziness again and Sean averted his eyes. In his haste he glanced down where the ground, two stories below, was also moving, and bobbing, and waddling about.

Big mistake, he thought, snapping his eyes shut. But it was too late. He felt himself falling backwards, his hands letting go of the railing. He flailed his arms and fell silently in slow motion.

"Whoa there Bucko!" he heard Slim Jim shout. "Just what do you think you're doing there now?"

"I'M FALLING!" Sean screamed, opening his eyes, at what was surely the last possible moment before hitting the ground, to find his hands still gripping the railing and his feet squarely on the top rung of the ladder.

* * *

"I'M FALLING!" shrieked the pudgy detective who stood on the ladder. *What is he talking about*, Raymond wondered. Was this guy tying to trick him? Trying to break his concentration?

Now this skinny cowboy was there telling him to "Drop it! Just drop it!" What the hell was he doing there? Why was he interrupting?

"Go away!" Raymond told him. "This is private."

The cowboy was just staring at him, hands out to his side, the fingers of one hand wiggling like he was ready to draw at a high-noon shootout. Raymond waved his hands and some of the birds took flight, spinning in a tight tornado-like vortex around the cowboy, blinding him with their bodies.

"Dag-nabit!" The cowboy shouted above the frenzied flapping of wings.

"Oh God!" Tia Lynn cried, sweet glimmering angel tears dropping from her chin. Tears Raymond wanted to wipe away. Tears he wanted to taste.

"It's okay," he told her. "We'll make them go away, and then we can talk."

* * *

Slim Jim's gun sounded three times. *CRACK! CRACK! CRACK!* The cyclone of birds spinning around him scattered, as did most of the pigeons on the roof.

There was a roar of flapping wings and Sean's field of vision went like static for a moment as everything was blotted out by dancing spots of black, grey, and white. When the swarm of birds cleared and he could see Slim Jim again, he saw that the detective had his revolver—that Remington six-shooter that was said to be a myth—trained on the little guy in the pigeon costume.

"Git down!" Slim Jim commanded. "Drop the hammer, and git flat on your belly!"

But the guy wasn't doing it. He had both hands up in the air, but he was still white knuckling the claw hammer, and was taking slow tentative steps backwards toward the edge of the roof. He was saying something, but he was talking to the girl, not Slim Jim, and Sean couldn't hear what he was saying over the noise and commotion of the panicked birds.

"Don't test me, Bucko!" Slim Jim yelled, stepping forward and squinting down the barrel of his pistol.

The little guy turned and his eyes flashed with crazy orange rings that made the flesh on Sean's neck go tight with goosebumps.

"You don't understand!" he was yelling. "You're just like that fucking exterminator, the one who murdered our chicks. The one who hit me. He was never going to understand. I'm sorry about what happened, I am, but he was never going to understand, never going to fit into the new world." He was waving the hammer at Slim Jim and spitting as he yelled. "But she does. She understands. And she'll tell you who I am, and what this means!"

He swung the hammer toward the girl. Slim Jim brought his other hand up to grasp the underside of his wrist, stabilizing his aim, and Sean knew that Slim Jim would do it, he would pull the trigger if this crazy fuck didn't drop that hammer right this very second. He wanted to scream out to the guy, tell him to do it, to drop it, but as he opened his mouth a roar of flapping wings drowned out his shout.

A dark blur of movement screamed out of the sky and crashed into Slim Jim, scores of pigeons smashed into him like kamikaze pilots. His body spun around, his knees went out from under him, and he dropped his gun as he tried to shield his face with his forearms. Birds continued to drop from the sky, to pummel him, many of them falling stunned or dead to the rooftop, as the cowboy pulled into a tight fetal ball. If he screamed or called out, Sean couldn't hear it over the frenzy of the birds.

Sean would never be able to explain exactly how his gun got into his hand, or if he warned the guy before squeezing off the four rounds that were missing from his magazine when the Internal Affairs investigators counted them, but he'd never forget seeing the guy's shoulder jerk, like he'd been shoved hard, when one of the bullets caught him just above the heart. The little guy stared with shocked orange-ringed eyes directly into Sean's eyes as he stumbled backwards. Dropping the hammer, he turned toward the girl, and in the sudden silence that followed the echoes of the four shots, Sean could hear him saying, "Tell them. Tell them that I was the one. I was the one!"

Sean thought maybe the guy would stumble off the roof, but he stopped at the edge and raised both arms, wincing against the pain as he held them out at his sides and turned his palms toward the swirling, angry sky. He closed his eyes and let his head fall limply back. Sean dropped his gun and rushed forward, reaching for the guy. But he was too slow, and was only able to watch as the guy in the pigeon costume took a deep, calm breath, and let himself fall backward off the roof.

The girl screamed, and then there was a sound like the roar of a waterfall as Sean looked over the roof's edge where the man fell into a dense swarm of birds who carried him up into the churning grey sky. The guy's little limp body tumbling like a ragged grey leaf caught up in the wind.

DIRT BIRD

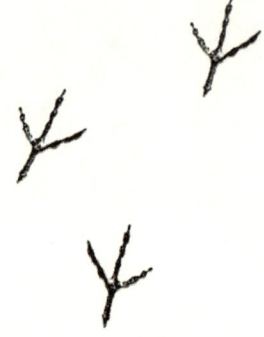

Raymond had never really been to the beach. He'd walked around in the sand at North Avenue Beach, the long stretch of Park District land that separated Lake Shore Drive and the Chicago skyline beyond from the small freshwater sea that was Lake Michigan, but he'd been there primarily to feed the birds, and had kept his shoes on. He had never been in water deeper than a bathtub, but somehow, what little bit of consciousness he clung to while he was carried through the low, dense cloud cover recognized that the continuous tossing and rolling of his body must have been much like the sensation of being caught up in the ocean tide. He was dimly aware of his body, as if it were far away, and only connected to him through faded sense memories. It tossed, and rolled, and rose, and fell without pattern or rhythm as its weight was haphazardly distributed by the tight swarm of birds around him.

He was surrounded, he knew, by thousands of his family members, yet for the first time since waking up in his nest, he felt utterly alone. He'd blacked out for an instant after the bullet had passed through his shoulder, and when he came to he was caught up in the tide of pigeons that was carrying him now, but something was different. He could no longer feel them. He could feel their talons gripping at every square inch of his coat, and at his harness, and at the laces of his boots. He could feel the lumps of their bodies as they swooped up and soared under him, letting him roll over their backs. But he could not feel their presence inside his head, or his inside of theirs. He could no longer see with their eyes, or hear with their ears. He could not flap their wings, and they could not coo his thoughts.

He was alone again, alone in the dark and falling…

* * *

Twenty minutes after the echos of Detective Sean O'Brian's four gunshots faded into the strange silence that fell upon the rooftop of that crooked little building, two F-16 fighters were scrambled from the Air National Guard Base at Springfield. Frantic calls had come from the towers at O'Hare, Midway, and Gary-Chicago international airports, each reporting an unexplainable smear-like radar anomaly, something much bigger than any known aircraft, moving southeast over the suburbs, and into northwestern Indiana.

* * *

Nelson had to take a little hop with every third step to clear the rows of soybean plants as he ran across the field toward the man the birds had brought.

Nelson had been jumping his remote controlled Jeep off the curb behind the gas station his mom worked at when he saw the cloud of birds drop out of the navy blue predawn sky like a slow-motion tornado. The sound of fifty thousand flapping wings was like the din of a million firecrackers going off in the distance. The dark cloud of birds, what kind of birds he couldn't tell, settled down on the immense, flat northern Indiana field behind the station like a swarm of giant locusts. They hopped, and fluttered, and waddled around for just a few moments, just enough time for Nelson to pick out the strange moist purring sound they made over the whine and sizzle of traffic on the interstate behind him. Then, as if on command, they all took to the air at once, leaving the shape of a man behind.

He was panting desperately and his chest burned by the time he'd covered the hundred yards and reached the man. The man was lying face up on one of the rows with his head resting in the relative softness of the bushy plants, and his arms and legs draped back on either side into the shallow rut between the rows. His eyes were closed and a dark wet patch of blood had soaked through the left shoulder of his raincoat. Nelson knew that your heart was on your left side, and figured the man must have been dead until he saw the man's stomach rising and falling with slow, shallow breaths. Nelson thought maybe he was a soldier because he had on black army pants, and red army boots, and one of those army suspender things you hung your gear and stuff on.

Nelson fell to his knees and reached out to touch the man's hand. It was cold like meat in the refrigerator.

He looked back over his shoulder. The sun was just beginning to rise behind the gas station, which was the only building in sight except for the shimmering silver silos of the farm that was at least half a mile farther away. He glanced around at the ground and saw lots of little three-toed bird tracks in the dirt between the rows, and a few feathers scattered here and there. He poked at the man once to see if his eyes would open. When they didn't, he got to his feet, turned around, and went bounding back over the field to tell his mom about the army man the birds had brought.

DIRT BIRD

Little Timmy tugged on Raymond's pant leg. "Grampa," the boy said, "you forgot to open your present."

Raymond smiled down on his youngest grandson, who pronounced his "R"s like "W"s. As tired as he was from the opening day festivities of his new gas station, he bent his old aching knees, and picked up the five-year-old.

"Hey there little chick! What are you doing up? Doesn't your momma ever put you to bed?"

The boy was holding the package Nelson had sent from Fort Lauderdale.

"Momma said I napped too much today, and that you should open Uncle Nelson's present."

Raymond set the boy on the counter next to the three brand new Slushy machines, each one churning it's own primary-colored concoction of ice and artificial flavoring, and took the package from his hands.

"Well, if your mamma says, then I guess I better, huh?" he said, kissing the boy on his forehead.

The round box was about the size of two small dinner plates sandwiched on top of each other and was sealed with red and white packing tape that read "fragile."

"Guess I'll have to be careful. What do you suppose it is?"

"A big cookie."

"Oh, I bet you'd like that, huh?"

Timmy grinned and nodded.

"But, see, your mistake is thinking that I would share my big ol' cookie with little ol' you." He poked the boy in the belly, making him burst into squirms and giggles.

"Open it!" Timmy demanded through his laughter, "Open it!"

The sand dollar had been wrapped in bubble-wrap and was in pristine condition. Bleached white, it was like a scalloped plaster pancake with five thin, oblong holes radiating unevenly from its middle. The little card taped to the flatter underside told "The Legend of the Sand Dollar" and said that the star pattern was a reminder of the star that led the wise men to the manger in Bethlehem, and that the flower-shaped marking on the more rounded top was either a peace lily or a Christmas poinsettia. Raymond had always thought it looked more like a marijuana leaf.

There was also a picture of Nelson, his wife Leeann, and Raymond's oldest grandson, Eddie, sitting around the table on their porch, which looked out over the pale blue waters of the Atlantic. Eddie, who was technically Raymond's step-grandson, was wearing his high school basketball jersey, and flashing a girl-catching smile of white teeth and a two-fingered peace sign. On the back, Nelson had scratched a few words with a blue ballpoint. They read:

> Dad,
> *Good luck with the new station. I'm sure it will be as successful as the other two.*
> *We love you.*

There was a squiggle Raymond recognized as his stepson's signature and a postscript that told him to, "Kiss Momma for me."

"You know what this is?" he asked Timmy, who was busy popping the little blisters on the bubble-wrap.

"A sand money."

Raymond shook the sand dollar. The tiny teeth of the creature rattled around in the skeleton. "Do you know what's inside?"

The boy nodded without looking up, "Doves."

Raymond shook his head, held the shell in both hands, and snapped it open, just like breaking a big cookie in half.

"Here," he said. "Hold out your hand." And he shook both halves, letting the five white teeth fall into the boy's soft little hand. They were tiny, no bigger than shelled sunflower seeds, and each one was a perfect little bird, its delicately feathered wings raised in a "V".

"See?" he said, pinching one of the birds with his thumb and finger, and holding it so his grandson could see, "They're beautiful white pigeons."

Timmy took one of the sand dollar teeth and held it up, squinting and imagining it as a bird in the sky.

"Do you know what pigeons are?" Raymond asked.

The boy brought the tooth close to the tip of his nose so he could study it. He smiled and used one of his little fingers to gently pet the bird he saw there. With each delicate little stroke the boy made a soft cooing noise.

Raymond put his arm around his grandson, the youngest of six, and hugged him. Timmy's head fell comfortably against his grandfather's chest as he smiled up at him and asked, "What are they Grampa?"

Raymond swallowed the lump that leapt to his throat and said, "They're angels, angels sent from heaven."

Coda:

The puzzling signal the air traffic control radars at O'Hare, Midway, and Gary-Chicago picked up was chalked up to an unidentified freak weather condition when it suddenly dissipated over Jasper County, Indiana. No connection was ever made between the anomaly, and the fact that, on the very next morning, Chicago woke up to find its entire population of pigeons missing. Most people didn't notice of course (how many pigeons did you see on your way to work this morning?), but the *Sun-Times* did run a small item in the Metro section of the following Sunday's edition. Dr. J. W. Prattle, of the Field Museum, was quoted as saying, "While I can not explain the strange behavior, I can say with relative certainty that the pigeon population was approximating normal numbers and distribution by the middle of that afternoon, and that no other strange behavior has been observed." By Monday it seemed to all that things were back to normal, and within days, the majority of Chicagoans had forgotten the matter entirely.

Thanks

There are a number of folks who supported me as I worked on this project that I want to thank. First I want to thank all of the friends and family who were willing to read early versions and give me feedback. Thanks to everyone who bought the digital edition, especially those who took the time to post reviews.

I owe a major debt to everyone in the Fiction Writing Department at Columbia College Chicago. The 12th floor is a magical place full of great people who helped me gather the courage to think of myself as a writer. There are a few folks I need to call out by name: Eric May, who pushed me to finish the first draft of this thing in a few short weeks, Gary Johnson, my trusted graduate advisor who never steered me wrong, and Randy Albers, captain of the 12th floor.

At the risk of name dropping I also have to thank Irvine Welsh for giving me a shot of confidence at a key moment.

Most importantly I need to thank Angela for...well, where do I start....

Wes Sturdevant is obsessed with story. His passion to become a storyteller led him from his hometown of Bloomington, Indiana, to Chicago where he studied at Columbia College Chicago and earned a BA in film production followed by an MFA in fiction writing.

Currently he is busy developing a number of graphic literature projects including the graphic novels *Distractions*, illustrated by Maza, (available now from Graphicly) and *Sins of Omission*, illustrated by Josh Johnson (slated for 2012). His first children's book, *Sleepy & Hollow and The Headless Horseman's Head*, a collaboration with illustrator Kris May, will be available for Halloween 2011. He is also working on other writing projects for both children and adults.

Wes lives in Indianapolis where his lovely wife, darling daughter, affectionate cat, and irrepressible three-legged mutt somehow find a way to tolerate his peculiar sense of humor.

You can connect with him and check out his current projects at www.storyandmedia.net